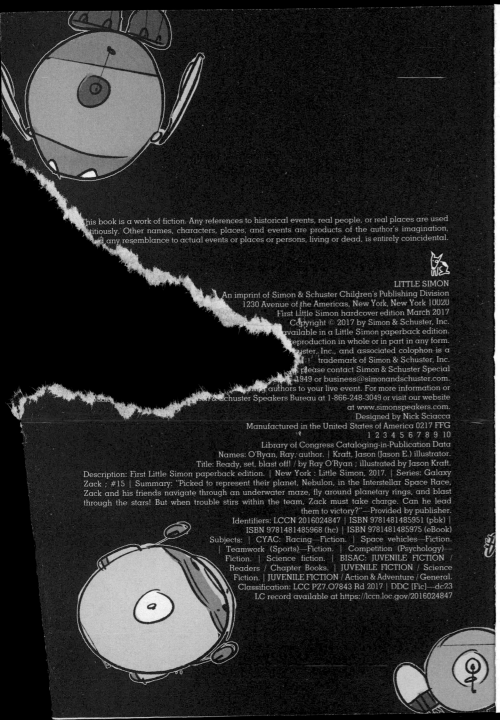

LITTLE SIMON
An imprint of Simon & Schuster Children's Publishing Division
1230 Avenue of the Americas, New York, New York 10020
First Little Simon hardcover edition March 2017
Copyright © 2017 by Simon & Schuster, Inc.
available in a Little Simon paperback edition.
reproduction in whole or in part in any form.
uster, Inc., and associated colophon is a
trademark of Simon & Schuster, Inc.
please contact Simon & Schuster Special
4949 or business@simonandschuster.com.
g authors to your live event. For more information or
chuster Speakers Bureau at 1-866-248-3049 or visit our website
at www.simonspeakers.com.
Designed by Nick Sciacca
Manufactured in the United States of America 0217 FFG
1 2 3 4 5 6 7 8 9 10
Library of Congress Cataloging-in-Publication Data
Names: O'Ryan, Ray, author. | Kraft, Jason (Jason E.) illustrator.
Title: Ready, set, blast off! / by Ray O'Ryan ; illustrated by Jason Kraft.
Description: First Little Simon paperback edition. | New York : Little Simon, 2017. | Series: Galaxy
Zack ; #15 | Summary: "Picked to represent their planet, Nebulon, in the Interstellar Space Race,
Zack and his friends navigate through an underwater maze, fly around planetary rings, and blast
through the stars! But when trouble stirs within the team, Zack must take charge. Can he lead
them to victory?"—Provided by publisher.
Identifiers: LCCN 2016024847 | ISBN 9781481485951 (pbk) |
ISBN 9781481485968 (hc) | ISBN 9781481485975 (eBook)
Subjects: | CYAC: Racing—Fiction. | Space vehicles—Fiction.
| Teamwork (Sports)—Fiction. | Competition (Psychology)—
Fiction. | Science fiction. | BISAC: JUVENILE FICTION /
Readers / Chapter Books. | JUVENILE FICTION / Science
Fiction. | JUVENILE FICTION / Action & Adventure / General.
Classification: LCC PZ7.O7843 Rd 2017 | DDC [Fic]—dc23
LC record available at https://lccn.loc.gov/2016024847

GALAXY ZACK

READY, SET, BLA[ST!]

By Ray O'Ryan

Illustrated by Jason Kraft

LITTLE SIMON

New York London Toronto Sydney New Delhi

CONTENTS

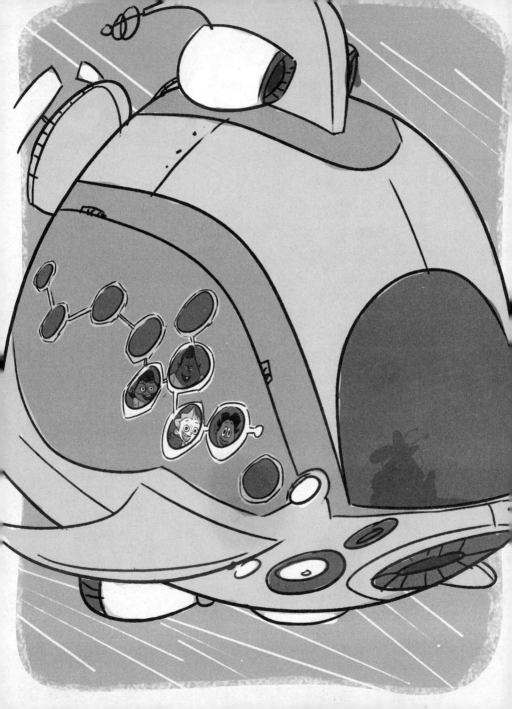

Chapter 1
The Zoomers

Zack Nelson stared out the window as stars zoomed by, twinkling brightly. Planets of every color, size, and shape filled the galaxy.

Zack loved space travel, especially with his friends. Any chance to be near stars made him happy.

He was sitting next to Drake Taylor. They had been best friends since Zack's family moved from Earth to Nebulon. Seth Stevens and Sally Zerbin sat behind them. Seth and Zack didn't get along when Zack first moved to Nebulon, but now they were good friends. Sally had been in Zack's idea group for the Intergalactic Science Fair.

He and his friends were going to Araxie, the water planet. They were in a racing club called the Sprockets Academy Zoomers. The Zoomers were picked to represent Nebulon in the Interstellar Space Race.

3

"Araxie is a really grape planet," said Zack. "I went there for vacation with my family and Drake."

"Yes, I learned how to swim right before that trip," Drake said. "Can you believe that I used to be afraid to swim? Now I love it."

"Me too," said Sally. "Araxie is the best place for swimming, diving, and riding astro-powered surfboards!"

4

Zack and Drake excitedly agreed.

Then Seth spoke up. "Well, there will be no swimming on this visit," he said. "I just want to win this race."

"We are going to do great in the races," said Drake.

"Yeah, we have a stellar team *and* the best spacecars. I can't wait to finally see the cars we designed in person," said Zack.

Everyone nodded in agreement. The team had spent weeks working on the designs for each car.

Then Zack's hyperphone began to ring. "It's my mom and dad," said Zack. He pushed a button and his parents' faces appeared on the screen.

"Hi, honey. Did you pack extra socks and shin guards?" his mom asked.

"Uh, Mom, we don't need shin guards," Zack explained. "I only wear those when I play hover-soccer."

7

"Well, make sure you buckle up and stay safe, Captain," said his dad.

"Don't worry, Dad. I always do," Zack said.

Zack knew his parents were worried. To be honest, he was a little nervous too. His friends had all competed in big races before, but this was his first time entering a racing championship.

Ms. Rudolph, Zack's teacher, tried to get everyone's attention. She was the team's chaperone.

"Mom, Dad, I have to go now," said Zack.

"Good luck, Zack," said Mom. "We love you."

"Get ready to blast off, Captain!" said Dad.

"Uh, right, Dad. Love you both too." Then Zack hung up his hyperphone.

"Okay, Zoomers, we are almost at Araxie," said Ms. Rudolph. "I know that you have all prepared for the race, but let's review the rules one more time."

Everyone quieted down and listened carefully.

"There are three wild rounds of competition," she explained. "The first round is here on Araxie.

10

You will be racing in the Aqua Track Underwater Maze. The second round will be on the planet Circulus. You'll compete on the Race Rings, ten gigantic rings that wrap around the planet. Then the final round will take place on the spectacular Magna Stella 4, where you will be racing through the famous Star Speedway."

"Yippee wah-wah!" Drake shouted.

"Sounds so grape!" agreed Sally.

They looked at one another excitedly as their teacher continued.

"The Stellar Robots pit crew will assemble each team's car before every round. The team cars will match the designs that you submitted earlier in the school year. Of course, your goal is to finish each course as quickly

as you can while avoiding any speed bumps. Speed bumps will freeze your car for a short time before you can continue. Are there any questions?" Ms. Rudolph asked.

"No, we are ready to race!" everyone cheered together.

"Okay, then. Zoomers, prepare for landing!" exclaimed Ms. Rudolph.

Chapter 2

Back to Araxie

"I cannot wait to speed through the Aqua Track!" said Drake.

"Yeah, this first race will be a piece of cosmic cupcake," said Seth.

"That is right," agreed Sally. "The first place trophy will be ours."

"You bet!" replied Drake and Seth.

Then they all laughed and gave one another a special team handshake.

Zack was happy to see his friends pumped for the race. He wanted to be as excited as they were, but the more he thought about the race the more anxious he became. He looked out the window as Araxie came into view.

The beautiful blue planet was almost completely covered in water. Zack was amazed by the thousands of tiny islands scattered across the ocean. He felt his nerves begin to calm down.

"There is the spaceport!" cried Sally.

"Look, it floats!" said Drake.

Right then a voice came over the space cruiser's sonic speakers with an announcement. "This is Captain Blurzok. We are about to land on Araxie. Please remain in your seats and fasten your seat belts."

18

There was a tall metal tower with a round landing pad on top. Zack watched as they safely touched down on the floating spaceport.

Ms. Rudolph led everyone off the cruiser and onto a hover-sailer just above the water. Zack watched as bright blue waves curled in the brilliant sunshine.

They soon arrived at a group of cabins that floated just above the water.

"We will be staying in these anti-grav cabins during our time on Araxie," said Ms. Rudolph.

Zack, Drake, Sally, and Seth were amazed by their cabins.

"Okay, Zoomers, we all need to get some rest," Ms. Rudolph reminded them. "Tomorrow is game time!"

Early the next morning, the Zoomers arrived at the Aqua Track. The track was filled with kids from all over the galaxy that were here to race. They were busy working with the Stellar Robots to put the finishing touches on their spacecars.

After Ms. Rudolph checked them in, the Zoomers walked around to look at the other spacecars. There was one that looked like a water bug and another one that looked like a seahorse. Zack really liked seeing what the other teams had invented.

Then finally they came to the spot
that was reserved for the Sprockets
Academy Zoomers.

"And now, the moment you've all
been waiting for. Here's your spacecar!" said Ms. Rudolph. "Wow, it really
does look like a jellyfish."

The round, curved shape looked like an open umbrella.

"That was the plan! It may look like a jellyfish, but it will race like a speedy submarine," said Zack with a smile.

The Zoomers climbed into the car as their teacher wished them good luck. Drake settled into the driver's seat.

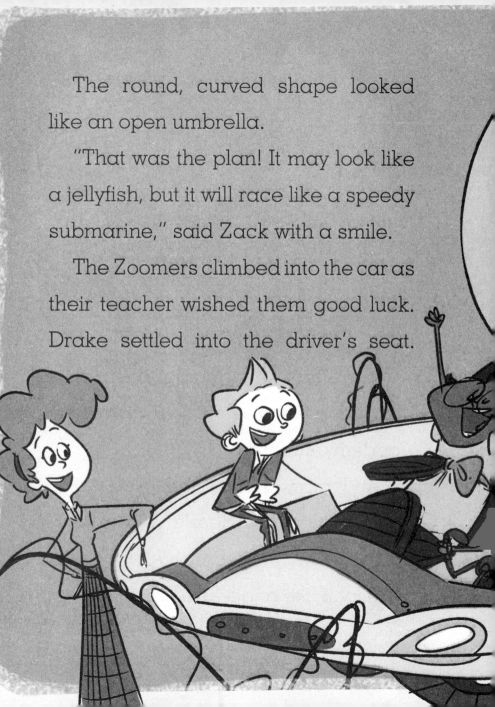

Then he shifted a rainbow dial to turn on the car. Lights flashed across the control panel as the spacecar dunked under the water. Zack looked down through the glass floor of the car. Rays of light extended deep into the ocean.

"The lights look exactly like jellyfish tentacles!" said Zack, delighted.

"Those light rays will give us extra hydro-boost in the water," Drake said.

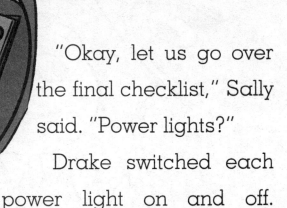

"Okay, let us go over the final checklist," Sally said. "Power lights?"

Drake switched each power light on and off. "Check!"

"Hydro-boost cylinders full?"

Seth checked all of the monitors. "Check!"

"Stellar harnesses on?" continued Sally.

"Check!" replied the boys.

"Emergency GPS activated?"

"Yes, activated," replied a voice.

"Wow, who was that? That sounds a lot like Ira," said Zack.

"I am Cara, your Car Automated Robotic Assistant. All preparations are finished," Cara confirmed.

"Cool," said Zack.

"Thanks, Cara," said Sally.

"Okay, Zoomers! Get ready to blast off!" Drake exclaimed.

Chapter 3
A-Maze-ing Race!

Each team eagerly waited as the start lights changed color.

Red, yellow, green! *Race time!*

The Sprockets Academy Zoomers were off! Drake instantly sped past a bunch of other teams.

The maze was made up of many

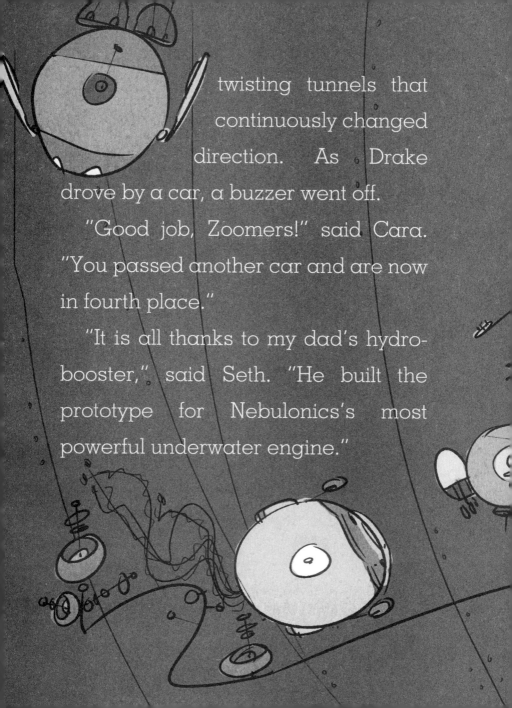

twisting tunnels that continuously changed direction. As Drake drove by a car, a buzzer went off.

"Good job, Zoomers!" said Cara. "You passed another car and are now in fourth place."

"It is all thanks to my dad's hydro-booster," said Seth. "He built the prototype for Nebulonics's most powerful underwater engine."

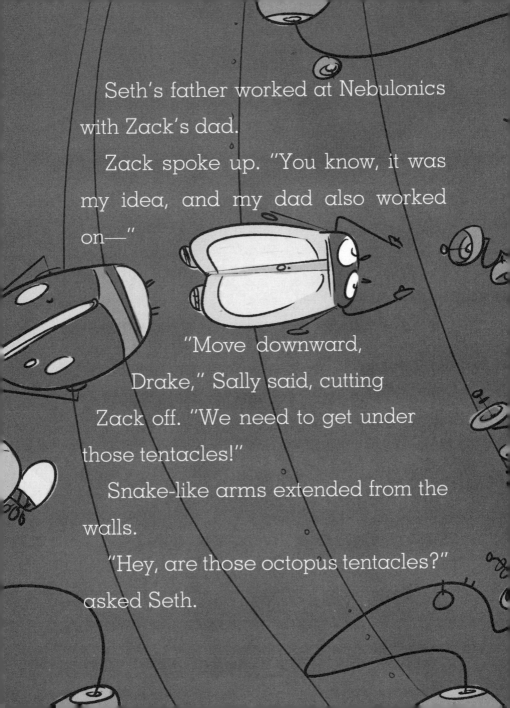

Seth's father worked at Nebulonics with Zack's dad.

Zack spoke up. "You know, it was my idea, and my dad also worked on—"

"Move downward, Drake," Sally said, cutting Zack off. "We need to get under those tentacles!"

Snake-like arms extended from the walls.

"Hey, are those octopus tentacles?" asked Seth.

"Yes, that is correct," said Cara. "They shoot out black ink that will freeze your car for five seconds."

"Okay. Hang on, guys!" said Drake as he steered the car down. Suddenly, a black cloud was released into the water. Drake took a sharp left to avoid getting hit.

"Good job!" cried Sally. "According to my nav-chart, we need to turn right at this corner and then make two lefts."

Drake lead the team through the maze exactly as Sally instructed. They continued to glide along when the buzzer went off.

"We are now in third place," said Cara.

"Only third?" muttered Seth. "We are moving as slow as a Gluconian slug."

Zack hoped that Drake didn't hear Seth. He tried to cheer on the team. "You're doing great, Drake. We moved up one ranking."

Drake started to fidget in his seat.

"Step on the hydro-boost pedal!" Seth yelled out, but Drake was too focused on the racetrack.

Damp sweat dripped down Drake's face as Sally calculated their next move.

"Here! Turn left here, now!" she called out.

Drake pushed hard on the brakes. The spacecar swung left and landed in front of a dead end. A jet of black ink shot from a waving tentacle.

"Oh no a speed bump!" cried Seth. "Now look what happened! We are frozen for five seconds!"

Cara counted down: "Five...four...
three . . ."

"Get ready to back up, Drake," said
Sally.

"Two . . . one!" Cara finished.

"Now!" exclaimed Sally.

Drake quickly backed up and turned
the car around.

"Step on the hydro-boost pedal," Seth repeated.

This time Drake heard Seth. He quickly zoomed ahead.

The buzzer went off again. "We are now in fifth place," said Cara.

"What? Fifth place? I—" Seth began.

Before he could continue, Zack interrupted as he pointed up ahead. "Look!" he cried. "It's the exit flag!"

"We can still make up for that speed bump. Time to turn on the rear igniters!" said Drake.

A burst of speed pushed them past three cars and across the finish line.

After a short pause, there was an announcement that blared out over the intercom. "Racers, in second place: The Sprockets Academy Zoomers!"

Chapter 4

On to Circulus

"Great finish, Drake!" said Zack.

"Yeah, that was grape!" said Sally.

"Yeah, nice recovery," said Seth. He seemed to be in a better mood.

"Thanks, you guys!" said Drake. He parked the spacecar in their lot as the robot pit crew helped.

Ms. Rudolph was waiting for them. She was so excited. "That was a great first round, Zoomers!" she said. "Your spacecar for the next round will be waiting for you on Circulus. Now let's go grab your things from the cabin

and head to the space cruiser. Next stop, the Race Rings!"

"This race will be tricky," said Sally. She studied the nav-chart aboard the space cruiser. "Circulus has ten rings that cross one another in all different directions."

"Not to worry—after all, *I* will be driving," said Seth. "You can sit back and enjoy the ride. I have got this under control."

"Sounds like a grape plan! Plus, the aerodynamic wings that Zack designed for this race course should really help," Drake said.

Zack smiled. He gave his friend a Nebulon handshake.

After three long hours, the Zoomers finally landed on Circulus. They immediately headed to the track to see their new spacecar. The Stellar Robots were busy installing a top wing.

"There are four wings—left, right, top, and bottom. That way, no matter which direction we are flying in, Seth will have control of the car," Zack explained.

"That is a fantastic idea," said Ms. Rudolph.

"Thank you," Zack replied with a smile.

"Yeah, but it is the driver who really counts!" boasted Seth.

Zack shrugged as Seth turned

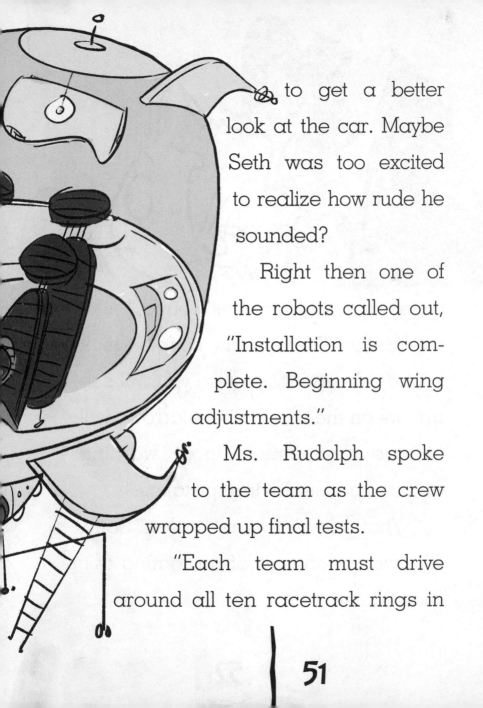

to get a better look at the car. Maybe Seth was too excited to realize how rude he sounded?

Right then one of the robots called out, "Installation is complete. Beginning wing adjustments."

Ms. Rudolph spoke to the team as the crew wrapped up final tests.

"Each team must drive around all ten racetrack rings in

order to complete this round," she explained. "It's not as simple as it sounds. As you fly around you will see arrows on the track. These arrows will change directions without warning and can cause driving mistakes."

"What do you mean?" asked Sally. She was in charge of navigating this race course too.

"The arrows show racers which direction they are allowed to drive," said Ms. Rudolph. "If you go the wrong way, you'll have to redo the entire ring again."

"Relax, Zoomers. I am the best at following directions," said Seth. "With me behind the wheel, we cannot lose."

Zack wasn't sure that Seth was right, but still he was relieved to not be driving. The Circulus ring course looked dizzying. *I'm happy being the team's engineer,* Zack thought.

As the robots finished working, Zack thoroughly inspected the spacecar.

"Everything looks good for the race tomorrow," confirmed Zack.

"Great! Now, is anyone else starving?" asked Drake.

The kids agreed as their stomachs growled, so Ms. Rudolph took them to the nearest diner before heading to their cabins for the night. They needed lots of energy for tomorrow's race!

Chapter 5

Ring around the Planet

The next morning, the kids waited anxiously at the starting line of the Race Rings.

"All systems ready," said Drake. "Round two on Circulus begins in thirty seconds."

"Navigation ready," said Sally.

"Wings are in position," said Zack.

Seth secured his stellar harness. "And pilot is ready!" he exclaimed.

The lights flashed until finally, they were off! They sped around the blue ring as the buzzer sounded out. Cara announced they were in first place.

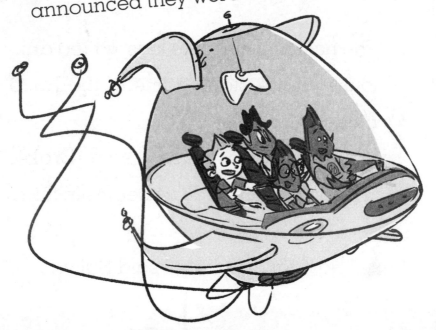

"Yippee wah-wah!" they all shouted.

"Watch this next curve," warned Sally as she checked her nav-chart. "This ring is very steep."

Suddenly, a left arrow appeared.

"Follow the arrow onto the next ring!" shouted Sally.

"I got it," said Seth. He switched into the left lane.

Just then an alarm went off beside Zack.

"What is that?" asked Drake.

Zack pulled up a vid-screen that showed the spacecar's engines. "It looks like engine one is overheating.

I'm going to switch us to engine two."

Zack put on his headset to communicate with the Stellar Robot crew for help.

Meanwhile, Sally kept her eyes glued to the arrow on the track. One mistake could cost them the race.

"I see the arrow, Seth! There it is! Go right!" Sally cried.

"We have to shift to the next ring!" shouted Drake.

"Will everyone please be quiet?" Seth asked. "Just let me focus."

"We were just trying to help," Sally said quietly as she slumped down in her seat.

When Zack finished switching the engines, he pulled off his headset. He could tell something strange had happened. Seth was focused on the road, but Drake and Sally seemed sad and were being extra quiet.

"What did I miss?" Zack asked.

The mood in the spacecar didn't feel like they were winning anymore. Drake told Zack what had happened. Sally was frowning with her eyes closed.

"Sally," Zack said, "don't let Seth get to you too much. Without you to give directions, the Zoomers would be stuck circling the rings forever!"

"Yeah, you are doing a great job!" added Drake.

She opened her eyes and smiled. "Thanks, guys. I just—" Sally gasped and pointed toward the ring field. All the direction arrows had disappeared from the path. The Zoomers were lost!

Chapter 6
Collision!

"Where did the arrows go?!" Seth yelled.

The buzzer went off several times.

"We are now in sixth place," Cara announced.

"What happened?" asked Drake. "We were just in first place."

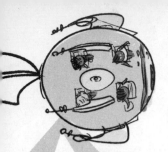

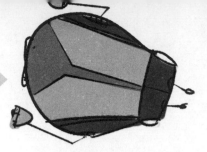

"I do not know," said Seth. "I have been watching the arrows like a Nebulon swoop bird. But the arrows switched and disappeared!"

Just then a car flew past them.

"We are now in seventh place," said Cara.

"Get with the program, guys!" Seth shouted. "Thanks for helping me . . . NOT!"

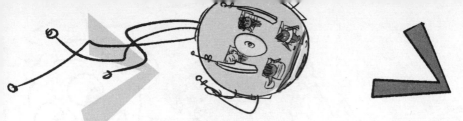

"Sorry, but we can work together now," said Zack.

Sally and Drake agreed as they all searched for their next arrow.

"There is one!" shouted Sally. The arrow was pointing backward.

"Throw the spacecar into reverse!" yelled Drake. "Now!"

Seth slammed down on the gears and steered the spacecar in reverse.

"How do we find the next forward arrow if it is behind us?" cried Drake.

"Sally, can you figure out which direction we need to go?" asked Zack.

"All arrows on the next ring should point forward," Sally said. "But we need to wait until the ring we are on connects with the next one. That is where we will find our next arrow."

"We need to switch rings now, or we will have to wait another lap before they line up again," said Drake.

"Got it. Do not worry, guys," said Seth calmly. "I have this under control."

As the rings drew closer to each other, Seth shifted the car forward. He was driving onto the next ring when another spacecar suddenly appeared in Seth's side-view monitor.

"Everybody, hold on!" yelled Seth.

CRASH!

Chapter 7
End of the Line?

The Zoomers' spacecar thudded to a sudden stop. The dashboard lights flickered off and then came back on again.

"Is everyone okay?" Seth called out.

"I am all right," said Drake.

"Me too," said Sally.

"Me three," Zack called out. "Good thing we were buckled up. Cara, status report, please."

"Two cars are down. Emergency mode has been activated," said Cara. "I have put up a protective force field around both cars. The other racers have been alerted about the accident.

Your teacher, Ms. Rudolph, will arrive with the Stellar Robots shortly."

Minutes later, the pit crew set up a safe-dome around the wreck. Ms. Rudolph ran to the Zoomer's spacecar.

"Students, are you all right?" their teacher asked.

"Yes, we are all okay. What about the team in the other car?" asked Drake.

"They're fine," said Ms. Rudolph.

"How bad does our spacec[...]
asked Seth as a Stellar Robot [...]
inside.

"The left engine is broken," the [...]
"Overnight repair is necess[...]
back to mech-room now."

"Wait, but what does that mean for us?" asked Sally.

"Unfortunately, thi_____
safe to drive," sai_____
you can't finish this_____
will have to sit this r____

said
Towing

"What? So do we lose?" asked Seth worriedly.

"Oh no!" said Zack. He looked at his teammates, disappointed.

"But this is not the end!" Ms. Rudolph assured them. "The official rules state that the final team rankings will be decided by adding up the two fastest times out of the three rounds."

"Does that mean we still have a chance to win?" asked Drake happily.

"We sure do!"

said Sally. "If we win the third race, then we can still take home the Interstellar Space Race first-place medal!"

"Yeah! The race isn't over until it's over," said Zack.

Drake and Sally cheered, but Seth just gave a faint smile as a tow-tractor beam pulled them off the course.

Chapter 8
Zack the Pilot

After traveling overnight, the Zoomers gathered at the spacecar port on Magna Stella 4. This planet was also known as the "star planet" because it was surrounded by the shining Star Speedway.

Zack, Drake, and Sally watched

as the Stellar Robots made the last adjustments to their car. The Star Speedway was made up entirely of tiny stars. To win the race, spacecars must fly from star to star. It was important to aim correctly because if they missed, they would get spun into space.

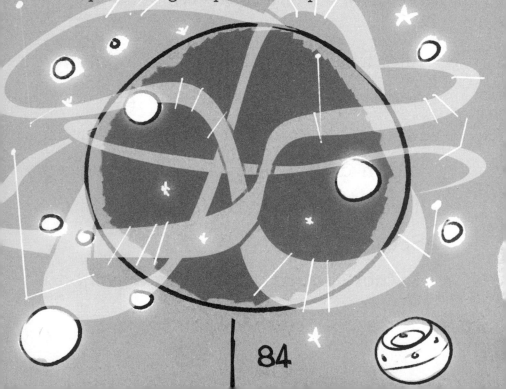

Seth joined them. He had not said a single word on the trip from Circulus to Magna Stella 4. "I cannot believe that we are in last place," he said.

"Well, we did not finish the last round," Drake pointed out.

"And I suppose that is my fault?" Seth snapped.

"Nobody is blaming you, Seth," Sally said.

"Rules are rules," said Drake.

Seth grumbled and walked away. Zack and Sally ran after him.

"Hey, cheer up, Seth," said Zack. "We all make mistakes. It's how you learn from them that makes you a champion. This competition isn't over yet, so don't count us out!"

"Plus, we saved the best spacecar for last!" said Sally.

The Zoomers all admired their cool new design.

"Look at the astro-powered hyper-jet engine with built-in ion blasters for extra speed," said Drake. "That was your idea, Seth."

"It was a great one, too," said Zack.
"C'mon, Seth, we're still a team, right?
Let's finish this race together."

Drake agreed, and Sally smiled too.

"I am sorry," said Seth. "I should not
have been so pushy before. You are
right, Zack. We are a team."

"Yeah!" the other Zoomers cheered.

"And," said Sally, "as a fellow team member, I think Zack deserves a chance to get behind the wheel!"

Zack immediately felt nervous. "What? But you were going to drive this round. I'm just the engineer."

"Go for it, Zack," said Sally. "You will do great. I know because with me directing, you cannot go wrong."

"Take us to the finish line, Captain!" said Seth.

Zack looked at his friends. Even though he was nervous, he knew he could not let them down. They all climbed into the spacecar. This time Zack settled himself into the driver's seat.

"Okay, let's do it!" said Zack. "Get ready to zoom to the stars!"

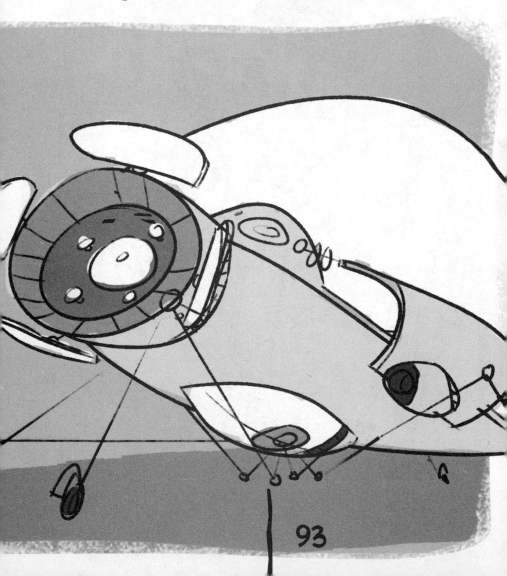

Chapter 9
Star Hopping

"Remember the Star Speedway rules," Ms. Rudolph said on their spacecar's monitor. "You must bounce from star to star to reach the finish line. Yellow stars will help maintain your speed. There are speed bumps, too. Flaming purple stars will spin you out of control.

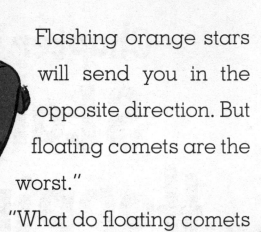

Flashing orange stars will send you in the opposite direction. But floating comets are the worst."

"What do floating comets do?" asked Zack.

"Well," Ms. Rudolph answered, "if you touch a comet by mistake, it will release a smoke cloud that freezes your ship in place. However, there are

also shooting stars that give you a one-minute power burst!"

"Moving into starting positions," Cara announced.

97

Zack took a deep breath. He felt his stomach tense as the spacecar tipped upward, aiming toward the stars.

"Good luck, Zoomers!" Ms. Rudolph said. "I'll see you at the finish line!"

The starting lights flashed as the sky twinkled above them.

Red, yellow, green! Race time! Zack stepped on the pedal, and the spacecar rocketed forward. "Wow!" Drake called out. "These stars are amazing!"

"I have never seen anything like it," said Sally.

Zack looked out the windshield at the bright course. He stared in awe as they passed by a speeding yellow star. Then he saw a purple star with

flames shooting from its surface. In the distance, he saw orange stars that blinked in and out.

Suddenly, a bright light streaked across the track.

"There is a shooting star!" Seth cried out. "Jump on it, Zack!"

Sally did a quick calculation on her nav-chart. "We need to increase speed and move higher!"

Zack pushed the pedal to the floor. They zoomed toward the shooting star as Zack steered the car higher. Soon the shooting star was right beneath them.

"Now!" cried Seth.

Zack went faster and headed right for the shooting star, but he missed the center landing spot. The spacecar shook with a jolt and started to fall.

"Um . . . I meant to do that," Zack joked as sweat dripped down his face.

Zack noticed a yellow star and quickly steered toward it. As soon as the spacecar bumped into the star, it bounced back into the race.

"Do not worry, Zack. There will be another shooting star," said Drake.

Zack relaxed. He could always count on Drake to keep him calm.

"And that chance is *now!*" shouted Sally. "There is another shooting star!"

Zack took a deep breath and flew straight at the shooting star.

"You are lined up perfectly," said Sally.

"We are going to make it!" said Drake.

106

Suddenly, the shooting star moved behind a floating comet! Zack tried to turn, but it was too late. Their spacecar was frozen in a cloud of comet dust.

Chapter 10

Team Zoomers

"What do we do now?" cried Drake.

"Cara, how long will we be frozen in place?" Zack asked.

"The comet cloud always lasts ten seconds," Cara replied.

"Ten seconds!" Seth shouted. "That is like *forever* in this race!"

"It is okay. Let us stay focused. We need to finish the course," Sally said.

Zack tried to breathe deeply and relax. The view from the spacecar was truly out of this world. Spirals of

purple and orange stars stretched into space, with other racers bouncing off yellow stars below them.

Hmm, purple and orange stars, thought Zack. "Hey, I have an idea, but it's a little crazy."

"We need a crazy idea to have any chance of winning," said Seth.

"Yeah, Zack, you are the captain," said Drake.

"How can I hit the corner of that purple star, Sally?" Zack asked.

"Oh wow," said Sally. "You are going to use the speed bumps to win the race! Yes, aim slightly left to hit the corner."

"Everyone, hold on!" said Zack as the comet cloud lifted and they dropped forward. The spacecar hit the purple star and spun out of control.

Then they hit another purple star and another and another. The Zoomers were bouncing wildly through the course. Buzzers were sounding off.

"We are passing racers!" cheered Drake.

Finally, the Zoomers bounced right into a flashing orange star, and instead of sending them backward, the star steadied the ship.

"Nice move, Zack!" said Sally.

"Yeah, brilliant idea!" said Seth.

"We are currently in sixth place," said Cara.

"Not for long!" said Sally. "There is another shooting star!"

Zack steered the car toward it, and this time hit the landing spot.

Their spacecar blasted forward, passing several other racers.

"There is the finish line!" said Drake.

Zack pushed down on the pedal with all his might and sped under the waving checkered banner.

There was a pause before Cara announced, "We have finished in third place."

"We did it!" cried Sally.

Seth smiled and gave his friend a pat on the back. "You are one good driver, Zack."

Zack smiled back and steered the spacecar toward their parking spot. "I'm only as good as my team, so that makes me awesome."

That afternoon, a big ceremony was held on Magna Stella 4. Zack's whole family came for the ceremony.

"Nice job, Captain!" said Zack's dad.

"We are so proud of you," said his mom.

Zack's twin sisters were happy for him too.

"You did a great job, Zack. We . . ."

". . . were surprised, but we . . ."

". . . knew you could do it!" sang
Charlotte and Cathy.

Zack beamed with pride.

Sally, Drake, and Seth's families were there too. Soon, the ceremony started, and everyone listened closely as the winners were announced.

"In third place for the bronze trophy are the Sprockets Academy Zoomers!" The crowd cheered as Zack, Sally, Drake, and Seth stood up.

"Nice job, guys," Zack said.

"Yeah, we may not have won gold, but we finished as a team," said Seth.

"That is the real prize," said Drake.

"And the trophy is just icing on the cosmic cupcake," said Sally.

They all celebrated as they stepped up onstage to receive their trophy.

HERE ARE SOME MORE OUT-OF-THIS-WORLD

GALAXY ZACK

ADVENTURES!